Reader's Clubhouse

THE CATERPILLAR

By Judy Kentor Schmauss
Illustrated by Mary Collier

BARRON'S

D0815829

Table of Contents

Illustrations on pages 21 and 23 created by Carol Stutz

All inquiries should be addressed to:
Barron's Educational Series, Inc.
250 Wireless Boulevard
Hauppauge, New York 11788
www.barronseduc.com

Library of Congress Catalog Card No.: 2005054862

ISBN-13: 978-0-7641-3286-5
ISBN-10: 0-7641-3286-5

Library of Congress Cataloging-in-Publication Data
Schmauss, Judy Kentor.
    The caterpillar / Judy Kentor Schmauss.
      p. cm. – (Reader's clubhouse)
    Summary: Illustrations and simple text follow a caterpillar through its metamorpho-
sis into a butterfly. Includes facts about butterflies, a related activity, and word list.
    ISBN-13: 978-0-7641-3286-5
    ISBN-10: 0-7641-3286-5
    (1. Caterpillars—Fiction. 2. Butterflies—Fiction. 3. Metamorphosis—Fiction.) I. Title. II.
Series.

PZ7.S34736Cat 2006
(E)—dc22

2005054862

Date of manufacture: 09/2009
Manufactured by: Kwong Fat Offset Printing Co., Ltd.
           Dongguan City, China

PRINTED IN CHINA
9 8 7 6 5

Dear Parent and Educator,

Welcome to the Barron's Reader's Clubhouse, a series of books that provide a phonics approach to reading.

Phonics is the relationship between letters and sounds. It is a system that teaches children that letters have specific sounds. Level 1 books introduce the short-vowel sounds. Level 2 books progress to the long-vowel sounds. This progression matches how phonics is taught in many classrooms.

The Caterpillar introduces the short "u" sound. Simple words with this short-vowel sound are called **decodable words.** The child knows how to sound out these words because he or she has learned the sound they include. This story also contains **high-frequency words.** These are common, everyday words that the child learns to read by sight. High-frequency words help ensure fluency and comprehension. **Challenging words** go a little beyond the reading level. The child will identify these words with help from the illustration on the page. All words are listed by their category on page 24.

Here are some coaching and prompting statements you can use to help a young reader read *The Caterpillar*:

- **On page 6, "up" is a decodable word. Point to the word and say:**

  Read this word. How did you know the word? What sounds did it make?

  Note: There are many opportunities to repeat the above instruction throughout the book.

- **On page 8, "lunch" is a challenging word. Point to the word and say:**

  Read this word. The caterpillar is eating at a special time. It rhymes with "crunch." How did you know the word?

You'll find more coaching ideas on the Reader's Clubhouse Web site: *www.barronsclubhouse.com.* Reader's Clubhouse is designed to teach and reinforce reading skills in a fun way. We hope you enjoy helping children discover their love of reading!

Sincerely,

Nancy Harris

Nancy Harris
Reading Consultant

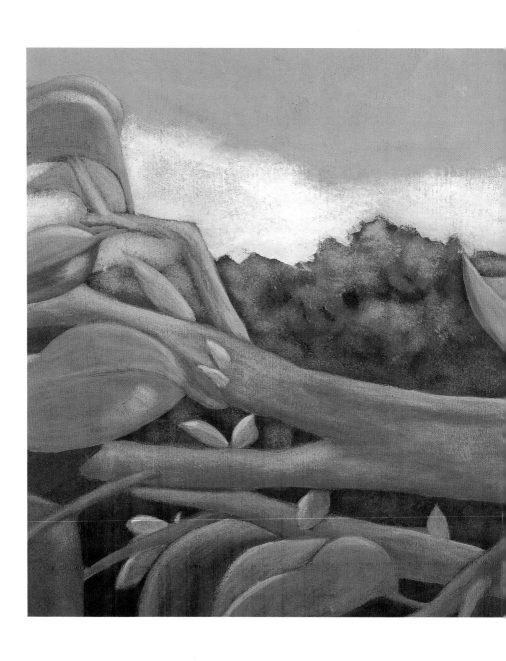

I am a caterpillar.

I can go up.

I can go down.

Look, I see my lunch.

My lunch is good. Yum, yum.

This is a good spot.
I am in luck.

I can bunk down here.

It is snug in here.
So snug.

I am snug as a bug in a rug.

The sun is up.

I can come out.

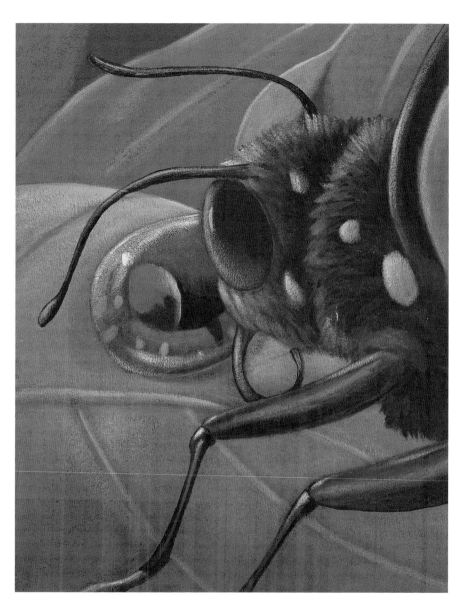

What am I now?

I am a pretty butterfly.

Fun Facts About
Butterflies

- At the end of the summer, more than 100 million monarch butterflies gather from all over the United States and Canada and travel south.

- Some monarchs travel more than 1,200 miles (1,931 kilometers) for 20 days to get to a warm place like Mexico!

- Monarch butterflies taste terrible to animals that want to eat them. That is how they stay safe.

- A monarch butterfly does not eat. It drinks nectar from flowers through its tongue. Its tongue works like a tiny straw.

• These are the main parts of a butterfly's body.

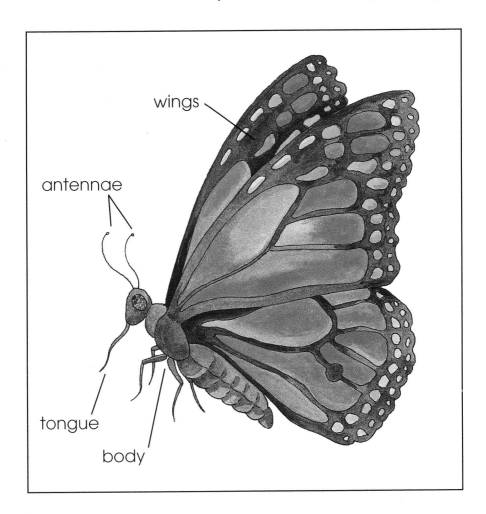

Life Cycle Mobile

You will need:

- three pieces of white construction paper
- safety scissors
- yarn or string
- a sturdy paper plate
- markers or crayons
- tape
- ruler

1. Decorate the paper plate using markers or crayons.

2. Draw the outline of a caterpillar on one piece of construction paper. Draw a cocoon on another piece, and draw a butterfly on the last piece. Color each picture and cut it out.

3. Cut three pieces of yarn or string the length of a ruler. Tape one end of the string to each picture.

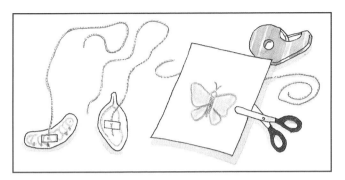

4. Tape the other end of each piece of string to the paper plate so the pictures will hang below the plate.

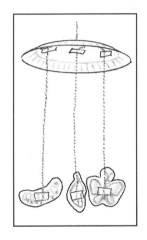

5. Cut another piece of string. Tape it to the top of the paper plate so the mobile can be hung from the ceiling.

Word List

Challenging Words	butterfly caterpillar lunch
Short U Decodable Words	bug bunk luck rug snug sun up yum
High-Frequency Words	a look am my as now can out come pretty down see go so good the here this I in is it